Smarty Marty's Got GAME

THIS BOOK IS DEDICATED TO MY LATE GRANDMA MARTHA.
I LOVED HOW MUCH SHE LOVED THE GAME OF BASEBALL.

Thank you to my sounding board, the ultimate fact checker and partner, my husband Paul. You've always encouraged me to try new things and challenge myself beyond what I considered my limits. I love you.

To my two beauties, Zachary and Gracie. Love doesn't begin to describe how I feel about you. You both make everything better by simply being in this world.

To my dad. Thank you for making sure I could play ball with the best of 'em. To my mom. Thank you for always letting me color in the diamond, in the scorebook and beyond. I love you both. —A.G.

FOR BRUCE BOCHY. —A.M.

The Giants Community Fund, a 501(c)(3) public charity, collaborates with the San Francisco Giants by using baseball as a forum to encourage underserved youth and their families to live healthy, productive lives. The Fund supports Junior Giants leagues throughout Northern California, Nevada and Oregon and provides assistance to targeted community initiatives in the areas of education, health and violence prevention.

Junior Giants, the flagship program of the Fund, is a free and non-competitive program serving 20,000 boys and girls, 5-18 years old. The goal is to reach kids who otherwise would not have the resources to play baseball, but more importantly the program provides a strong curriculum and well-trained volunteers to work with youth to develop life skills. For more information please visit jrgiants.org.

A portion of the proceeds from sales of Smarty Marty's Got Game will be donated to Junior Giants.

Text copyright © 2013 by Amy Gutierrez

Illustrations copyright © 2013 by Adam McCauley

Edited by Amy Novesky, www.amynovesky.com

Book design by Sara Gillingham Studio, www.saragillingham.com

Printed in China.

Library of Congress Control Number 2013941449   ISBN 978-1-937359-51-5

Cameron + Company
6 Petaluma Blvd., Suite B6
Petaluma, CA 94952

www.cameronbooks.com

Second Printing

SMARTY MARTY'S
Got
GAME

BY

AMY GUTIERREZ

ILLUSTRATED BY

ADAM McCAULEY

It was the day of the **BIG GAME.**
Marty and her little brother Mikey had tickets.

Marty loved baseball. Her nickname at school was
SMARTY MARTY, because she knew more about the game
than anyone.

"It's called America's Pastime, because before there
were video games, people used to play baseball
to pass the time," Marty told Mikey.

Mikey did not like baseball one bit. Baseball was **LONG.**
Baseball was **BORING.** Baseball was no video game.

Marty got her love of baseball from her Great Grandma Martha (Gigi), who loved baseball **MORE THAN ANYTHING.** Gigi followed the game faithfully and even kept her own scorebook. She taught Marty everything she knew.

Mikey never got a chance to know his great grandma. So today Marty was going to teach him everything Gigi had taught her.

It was time he learned why baseball was the

GREATEST GAME

in the world.

At the ballpark, the sky was blue and the sun was bright. Marty was wearing her lucky cap.

"IT'S HOT," complained Mikey.

Marty put a brand-new cap on Mikey's head.

"I'M HUNGRY."

"Ballpark food is the best," said Marty.

Marty and Mikey started with garlic fries. But there was so much to eat! Cha cha bowls and pretzels, hot dogs, popcorn, nachos, and churros for dessert.

MAYBE BASEBALL WASN'T SO BAD,

thought Mikey, his belly full.

Marty and Mikey took their seats right before the ceremonial first pitch. MARTY LOVED THE FIRST PITCH. It meant the game was about to begin.

"If the ball hits the ground before home plate, you boo because they 'BOUNCED IT,' and if the ball hits the catcher's glove, you cheer."

Mikey watched as the fan started her windup, threw the ball, and BAM!—hit the catcher's glove.

"STRIKE!" yelled Marty. Mikey cheered.

At the top of the first, Marty had a surprise for her little brother—THE SECRET TO MAKING BASEBALL FUN. She pulled out her special scorebook. "Wanna help me keep score?"

Mikey never thought Marty would share her most valuable possession. By the end of the first inning, Mikey had learned the basics of the game.

PLAYERS		1	2	3	4	5	6	7	8	9	10	11
LF	#8 Zachary Gutierrez											
SS	#9 Pablo Segura											
3B	#16 Bobby U. Fullerton											
1B	#32 Henrique Gomez											
CF	#12 Michael Roberts											
RF	#17 Jaime Segura											
2B	#3 Johnny Cleveland											
C	#5 G.K. Smoove											
SP	#90 Al Papas											

Nine players each play a numbered position.

Every player has a job, and it is the manager's job ("*NEVER CALL HIM 'COACH'!*") to decide who plays where. The manager also decides the order in which the nine players will hit.

Hitters one and two are "TABLE-SETTERS." Their job is to get on base.

Three, four, five and six are POWER HITTERS, and they often hit home runs.

Seven and eight are "BACK END" of the lineup.

The pitcher almost always bats last and is a good bunter.

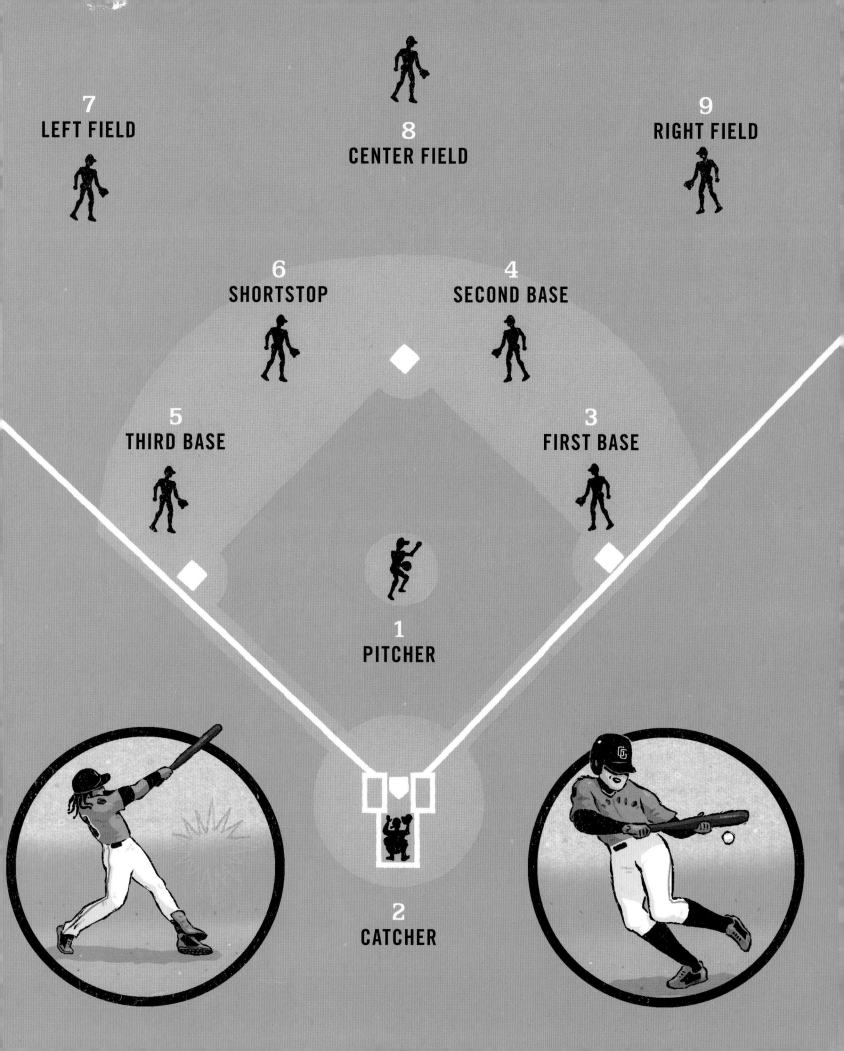

"BUNTING IS SILLY," said Mikey. "The guy always gets thrown out at first."

Marty's eyes went wide, and she took a deep breath. "Bunting," she said, "is actually VERY IMPORTANT."

Usually it's about giving up a turn to bat so that a teammate can move to the next base.

And yes, the runner was thrown out at first, but both runners on base advanced and were now in

SCORING POSITION!

CRACK! BAM! POW!

The Good Guy smashed the ball into the outfield. It was caught, but the crowd still went wild.

"Why is everyone cheering?" cried Mikey. "He's out."

"Ahhh, the sacrifice fly!" said Marty. "It's kind of like a bunt, but more exciting! The batter hits a HIGH AND DEEP FLY BALL that will be caught, but it gives his teammate enough time to TAG THE BASE AND RUN HOME TO SCORE."

OTHER GUYS	0	0	0	0	0	0	0	0	0		0
GOOD GUYS	0	1	0	0	0	0	0	0	0		1

For the next few innings Mikey helped
Marty score the game. Scoring did make
baseball a bit more fun.

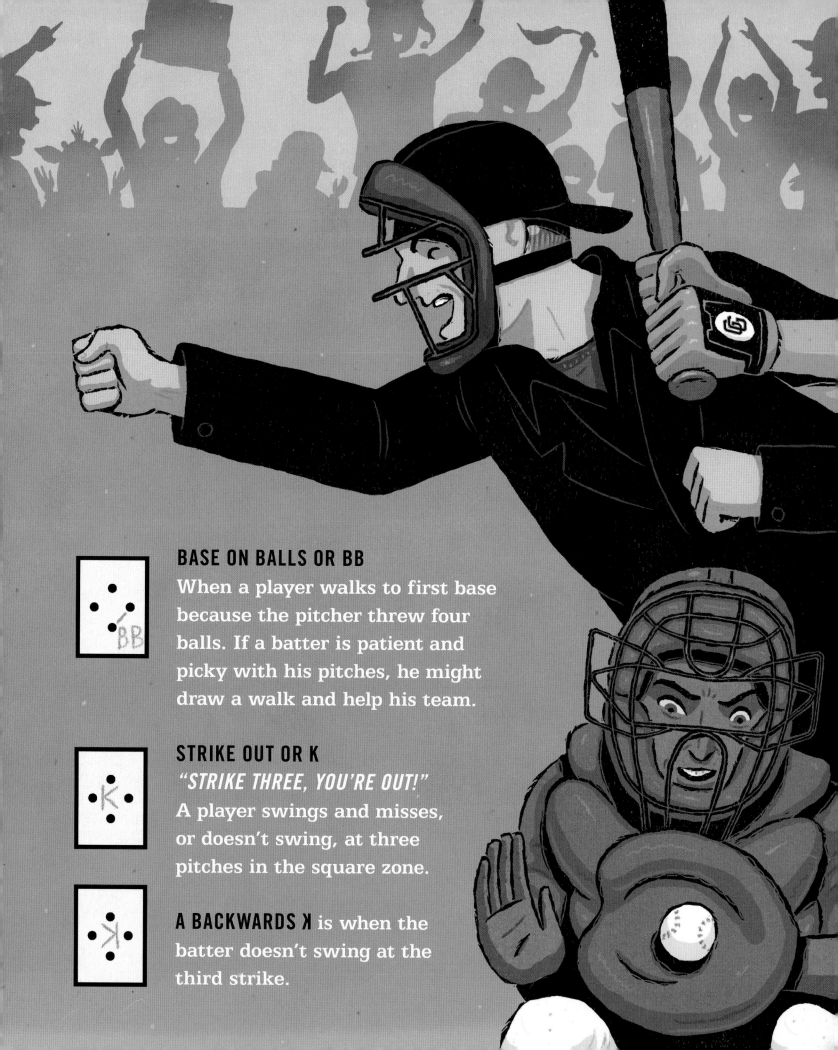

BASE ON BALLS OR BB

When a player walks to first base because the pitcher threw four balls. If a batter is patient and picky with his pitches, he might draw a walk and help his team.

STRIKE OUT OR K

"STRIKE THREE, YOU'RE OUT!"
A player swings and misses, or doesn't swing, at three pitches in the square zone.

A BACKWARDS ꓘ is when the batter doesn't swing at the third strike.

1 0 0 3
2 0 0 4

DOUBLE PLAY OR DP
When two outs are made in one play. 6-4-3 is most common.

DP
6-4-3

TP
5-4-3

5-4-3 is called "AROUND THE HORN."

SINGLE (1B)
1B

DOUBLE (2B)
2B

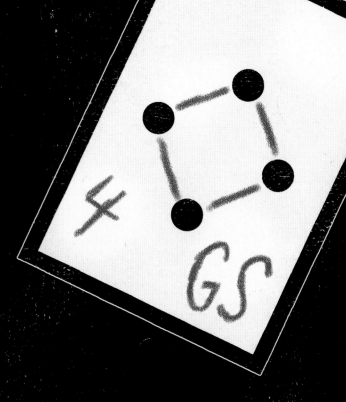

TRIPLE (3B)

GRAND SLAM (GS)

HOME RUN (HR)

The crowd stood up and cheered as the starting pitcher made his way back to the mound.

THE "ACE" was the best pitcher on the team, and pitching into the ninth inning meant he was having a great game.

When the first batter struck out, Marty yelled,

"GRAB SOME PINE, MEAT!"

just like one of her favorite announcers.

The batter had to go back to the dugout and sit on the bench.

With a one-run lead, the Good Guys' manager tapped his left arm, and a new left-handed pitcher came in. The closer threw the ball hard and fast and usually "closed out" the game . . . BUT NOT TODAY.

The Other Guys scored and tied the game.

In the bottom of the ninth, tied at three-all, the home team had "last licks." Mikey found himself on the edge of his seat. Three hours had flown by.

"LET'S DO THIS," he said through gritted teeth.

"STRIKE ONE!" yelled the ump.

Mikey closed his eyes tight, then opened them ever so slightly as the pitch crossed the plate.

"STRIKE TWO!"

Mikey covered his face with his hands and watched the next pitch through his fingers. Marty knew exactly how Mikey was feeling. It was the same feeling she had when she first started watching baseball with Gigi.

BASEBALL WAS EXCITING.

WHACK!

The Good Guys crushed the ball.
Marty and Mikey watched it soar.

Marty mimicked her other favorite announcer:
"HE HITS IT HIGH! HE HITS IT DEEEEEEP!

"IT IS *OUTTA* HERE!"

The stadium erupted. Fans hugged. Mikey and Marty jumped up and down. The home team had won on a walk-off home run.

They rushed out of their dugout whooping and jumping.

Marty's favorite part of scoring a game was coloring
in the **WINNING** home run diamond. She carefully moved
her pencil around the horn, and decided it was time
for her own sacrifice fly.

"Wanna color it in?" she asked Mikey,
handing him the pencil.

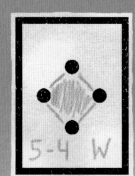

Mikey shaded in the diamond.

"Marty?"
"Mikey?"
"Whaddya know about football?"

Marty looked up to the sky, where that beautiful walk-off home run was hit. She smiled and tipped her lucky cap to Gigi.

AUTHOR'S NOTE

My grandmother passed away on November 12, 2012. The SF Giants had just won the second World Series in three years. When I was asked to ride in a car during the celebratory parade on Halloween, no one was more excited than my Grandma Martha, who was at home with hospice. Born in Ohio, she grew up an Indians fan, and when she and my grandfather moved west she became a diehard LA Dodgers fan. I know, I know—but it really was her only flaw.

My grandparents moved from Southern California to Petaluma nearly twenty years ago, and she slowly came around to root for the men in orange and black. We visited and spoke on the phone with regularity and never had a conversation without talking ball. She watched nearly every game, always calling me beforehand to check what time I'd be on TV. She liked to see me on television, but she LOVED watching baseball. This book only expresses a portion of how I felt about her. I'm so fortunate to have had forty years with a woman who never met a stain she couldn't get out and could have put together a lineup to rival any manager in the game. She really was Smarty Marty.

If you're wondering how I learned to score, it was from yet another female who played a role in the male-dominated world of baseball. It seems like I spent my entire childhood at the Little League field. My brother played, my dad coached, and my mom kept score. I'd sit next to Mom (not realizing I was receiving career training) and watch her make the marks in the book, each slash of the pencil having its own meaning. The ultimate moment coloring in the diamond when a run crossed the plate. I don't know if she knew then how much I loved keeping score with her. It made me feel like I had a role, win or lose. She knows now.

So I guess, looking back on my life, it doesn't seem so strange I ended up with a career in baseball. I love what I do and I hope this book finds its way into your hearts, as it came straight from mine.

—Amy G.

SMARTY MARTY'S
SCORECARD
TIPS

- **USE A PENCIL,** 'cause you'll make mistakes!

- **HAVE EXTRA PENCILS** in case you break one in frustration when your team's not doing well!

- **START SIMPLE.** Don't try to score everything. As you get better, add more to the cards.

- **USE SYMBOLS THAT MAKE SENSE TO YOU.** There are no rules for scoring a game, and everyone has their own style. For example, what kind of mark would help you remember a pitching change?

- **USE THE RESOURCES AROUND YOU AT THE BALLPARK:** your neighbors keeping score and the stats on the scoreboard (runs, hits, errors, pitch count, strikeouts), etc.

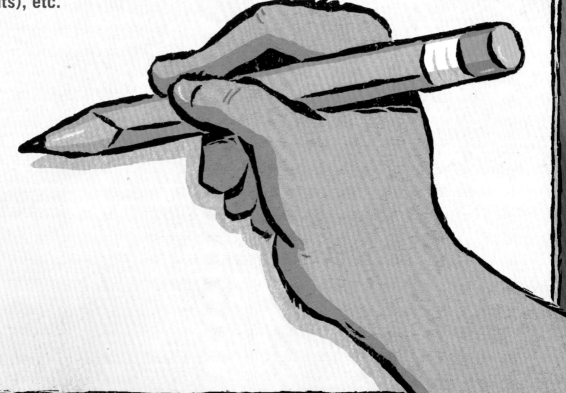